PARENT AND
TESTIMONIALS

"Kids will love the riddles, brain teasers and knock-knock jokes in this book!! Lots of laughter and good, clean fun await you. I'm a Grandmother, and I can hardly wait to read this to our grandkids!!"

~Dr. Becky Slabaugh #1 International Bestselling Author, Keynote Speaker, Licensed Clinical Pastoral Counselor, Mother of 2 Sons and Grammie to Tatum and Maisy Grace."
www.InnerTreasuresMinistries.com

"Although this book was written for children, it is also an excellent stress reliever for adults! It can be read by anyone who wishes to lighten up his or her mood. Jackie Morey is a mother of two young children and she knows how to spend quality time with her children telling jokes, solving riddles and

brain teasers, or doing word searches. Co-written with her son Michael, the activities in this book were written through the eyes of a joyful child."

~Rowena Arrieta, World-class International Classical Pianist, Finalist and Laureate at the VII Tchaikovsky International Music Competition, Mother of two.
http://bit.ly/RowenaArrietaPianist

"What a cool and fun book this is!! Riddles, brain teasers, tongue twisters and knock-knock jokes all in one place!! If you're a parent, grandparent or someone who's around kids, you'll want to get this book to read to them. And you might find yourself chuckling a bit as well. Perfect birthday gift, too."

~Matt Buchanan, Operations Manager, Father of 4, Grandfather of 10, and Great Grandfather of 2.

My 4 grandchildren (ages 9,8,5 and 4) absolutely love jokes! And this book is full of good, clean jokes and riddles! As a very committed and intentional Grandmother I'm always looking for age appropriate resources and books to read and enjoy with my four Grandbabes. This book 100% fits the bill! I plan to give it away as birthday gifts for all the families I know with children.

~Sharon Best, Mother of two, Grandmother of four, Life Coach

THE AMAZING BOOK OF RIDDLES, JOKES, KNOCK-KNOCK JOKES AND BRAIN TEASERS

Your BONUS for checking out this book: Jackie and her business friend Jay Boyer did a webinar in November 2017 called "**How to Write and Publish a #1 Bestselling Children's Book in 7 Days or Less.**" Please go to this link to watch the Replay: http://bit.ly/ChildrensBookJackieMorey

Quick note: Although the Bonuses mentioned in the webinar have already *expired*, the webinar content is value-packed **and** as relevant today as it was then. If you've always wanted to write a Children's Book, **this** is the webinar to watch right now http://bit.ly/ChildrensBookJackieMorey

And whenever you're ready **and** are serious about writing your Children's book, invest in yourself and learn from Jay Boyer who's a Children's Book Bestselling Author http://bit.ly/cbf-jackie

The Amazing Book of Riddles, Jokes, Knock-knock Jokes and Brain Teasers

Loads of FUN, Smiles and Laughter
for Kids, Friends, Parents,
Grandparents and Relatives

JACKIE MOREY AND
MICHAEL MOREY

Published by

Customer Strategy Academy, LLC
16212 Bothell Everett Hwy, Suite F111
Mill Cree, WA 98012
Author Jackie Morey's email:
CustomerStrategyAcademy@gmail.com

As of this publication, Michael's age is less than 2-digits – so if you wish to connect with Michael, please do so only via his Mom's email address above. Thank you.

Limits of Liability and Disclaimer of Warranty

The authors and publisher shall not be liable for the reader's misuse of this material. This book is for strictly informational and educational purposes.

Disclaimer

The views expressed are those of the author and do not reflect the official policy or position of the publisher or Customer Strategy Academy.

Copyright Use and Public Information

Unless otherwise noted, images have been used according to public information laws.

Paperback ISBN: 978-1-7332501-0-8

JACKIE'S DEDICATION

To my extraordinary Husband Jim – who is incredibly witty, topnotch at puns, and enjoys making me laugh right before bedtime, causing me to roll on the floor laughing!

To our two children – Michael and Alyssa – who both thoroughly enjoy jokes, riddles, knock-knock jokes and brain teasers! Remember that having a cheerful heart is good for everyone (Proverbs 17:22), and I've enjoyed sharing these jokes and riddles with you.

And to my parents, siblings, all my nephews and nieces, to our extended families, and to all my friends in the U.S., and all over the world who love to laugh. I hope you enjoy this book! And I invite you to invest in at least 10 more to give away to the many kids in your life who love to laugh and enjoy good, clean fun!

MICHAEL'S DEDICATION

To my sister Alyssa, my Mom and Dad, Tito Wes & Tita Cherry who gave me my first 4x4 Rubik's cube, to the Pineda Family, the Lansangan Families, the De Guzman family, my Grandpa and Grandma in the Philippines, to all my relatives, all my teachers, and all my friends – especially Joseph, Roman, Cameron, Cooper, Jeremy, and Jola.

And to all the kids and grownups in the world who want to laugh out loud with their friends and family.

Table of Contents

CHAPTER 1

Riddle Fun

1. What goes up but never comes down?

   Answer: A person's age

2. What is black and white and "red"
   (homonym of read) all over?

   Answer: A newspaper

3. What is black and white and red all over?

   Answer: An embarrassed zebra

4. What is black and white and red all over?

   Answer: An embarrassed Mickey Mouse

5. What is black and white and red all over?

    Answer: An embarrassed Orca

6. What is black and white and red all over?

    Answer: An embarrassed Penguin

7. What is green and brown and white all over?

    Answer: An evergreen tree covered in fresh snow.

8. You buy me to eat, but never eat me?

    Answer: silverware

9. What is dark but darkness eliminates it?

    Answer: A shadow

10. What is red like blood, gooey like glue, and tasty like salt?

    Answer: Ketchup (or Catsup)

11. What is stretchy, colorful and filled with air?

    Answer: A balloon

12. What flies when it's alive, lays somewhere when it's old and runs when it's dead?

Answer: A snowflake

13. What is a type of shoe, but not a shoe?
Answer: Sandals

14. What type of glass can tell time?
Answer: An hourglass

15. What has hands but can't clap?
Answer: A clock

16. Why does a milking stool only have 3 legs?
Answer: Because the cow had the udder one

17. Why does a flamingo stand on one leg?
Answer: Because it would fall over if it lifted the other one.

18. What helps children, but children throw them away for good?

    Answer: Used Pencils or used pieces of paper

19. What helps people see, but it goes on ears?

    Answer: Eyeglasses

20. What man is all dressed up but never moves?

    Answer: A snowman

21. What is white as snow, but not snow, and is as fine as sand, but not sand?

    Answer: Salt

22. Why are pigs terrible at basketball?

    Answer: Because they're always hogging the ball.

23. What do people stand up for, but is not alive?

    Answer: Flag

24. What has a face, but no eyes, nose or mouth?

Answer: A clock

25. What is full of holes but can still hold water?

Answer: A sponge

26. What is between the ground and the sky, and if anyone tries to get closer, it only goes farther?

Answer: The horizon

27. What does an angry stomach do?

Answer: It growls.

28. Which letter of the alphabet has the most water?

Answer: C (sea)

29. What word begins and ends with an E, but only has one letter?

    Answer: Envelope

30. What kind of cup can't hold water?
    Answer: A cupcake

31. It comes down but never goes up. What is it?
    Answer: Rain.

32. What type of dress can never be worn?
    Answer: An address

33. This kind of coat you can only put on when wet. What is it?
    Answer: A coat of paint

34. It flies around all day but never goes anywhere. What is it?
    Answer: A flag

35. This goes up and down but never moves. What is it?
    Answer: A flight of stairs.

36. It has a neck, but no head, and it wears a cap. What is it?

    Answer: A bottle.

37. What always sleeps with its shoes on?

    Answer: A horse

38. Why do dragons sleep all day?

    Answer: Because they like to hunt knights. (Sounds like nights)

39. What key can never open doors?

    Answer: A donkey

40. What can honk without a horn?

    Answer: A goose

41. What type of animal in the animal kingdom describes how it makes people feel?

    Answer: Bugs

42. What has a horn but does not honk?

    Answer: A rhinoceros

43. Which month has 28 days?

Answer: All of them.

44. What is a big as an elephant but weighs zero pounds (or zero kilograms)?

Answer: The shadow of an elephant.

45. What has bark but no bite?

Answer: A tree

46. What has lots of limbs, but never walks?

Answer: A tree

47. What can clap with no hands?

Answer: A thunder clap

48. What bet can never be won?

Answer: The alphabet

49. What travels all around the world but stays in one corner?

Answer: A stamp

50. What gets beaten and whipped but never cries about it?

Answer: An egg

CHAPTER 2

Jokes

1. Why did the boy take a sketch pad and pencil to his bedroom?

    Answer: So that he could draw his curtains.

2. What did one candle say to the other candle?

    Answer: I'm going out tonight.

3. Who owned most things on earth during the days of Abraham? (Bible-based riddle and play on words)

    Answer: Lot. Because he had a "lot."

4. Who had the most animals at one point in history? (Bible-based riddle.)

   Answer: Noah

5. Why does the math book feel sad?

   Answer: Because it has so many problems.

6. What did the boy say to the bug that bit him several times?

   Answer: Stop bugging me!

7. What do you call a naughty monkey?

   Answer: A Bad-boon

8. What do you call an exploding monkey?

   Answer: A Ba-boom

9. Why did the bumblebee put honey under his pillow?

   Answer: Because he wanted to have sweet dreams.

10. Why did the skeletons not watch a horror movie?

    Answer: They had no guts!

11. How do the skeletons who live far from each other communicate?

    Answer: A Cell bone

12. What did one eye say to the other?

    Answer: Don't look now, but something between us smells!

13. What did the egg say to the funny, joke-telling baker?

    Answer: You crack me up.

14. What did the funny, joke-telling baker say to the cake?

    Answer: The yoke's (play on words: joke's) on you!!

15. Why did the bread go to the doctor?

    Answer: He felt crumby (crummy)

16. Why did the robber take a shower after he robbed a bank?

    Answer: He wanted to have a clean getaway!!

17. What do you call a cashew in space?

    Answer: An astro-nut (play on words: astronaut)

18. What did the hungry horse say to the other hungry horse?

    Answer: Hey, look – there's hay!!

19. Why are Dogwood trees loud?

    Answer: Because they have a lot of bark.

20. Why do burglars wear striped shirts?

    Answer: Because they don't want to be spotted.

21. Why did the boy bring a ladder to his middle school?

    Answer: Because he wanted to go to high school.

22. What do you get when you cross a calf and a tear drop?

Answer: A cafeteria (play on words)

23. What did the ocean do to the man?

Answer: The ocean waved.

24. What has to be broken before you can use it?

Answer: An egg

25. What did the water say to the boat?

Answer: Nothing. The water simply waved.

26. If everyone bought a white car, what would we have?

Answer: A carnation. (Car-nation)

27. Where does Friday come before Thursday?

Answer: In the dictionary.

28. Mary's father has five daughters – Nana, Nene, Nini, Nono. What is the name of the fifth daughter?

Answer: If you answered Nunu, you're mistaken. It's Mary, of course.

29. What occurs once in a minute, twice in a moment and never in one thousand years?

Answer: The letter M.

30. Throw away the outside and cook the inside. Then eat the outside and throw away the inside. What am I?

Answer: Corn on the cob – you throw away the (outside) husk, cook the inside – the corn itself, then eat the (outside) kernels and throw away the (inside) cob.

Bonus Joke: One afternoon, the pilot of a small private plane took a lawyer, a priest and a young kid, flying high above the countryside. The plane began having engine trouble. In spite of doing his best to fix the airplane problem, the pilot couldn't. He quickly told all his passengers, "I have a wife and kids. I deserve to live. You all bail out, too." There were only 3 parachutes in the plane. The pilot quickly put on one parachute and jumped out. The lawyer arrogantly declared, "I'm one of the smartest men in the world and I deserve to live!" He grabbed a parachute and jumped out. The priest immediately told the young kid, "Kid, grab this parachute and let's bail out. You and I will be just fine. One of the smartest men in the world just jumped out with my backpack!"

CHAPTER 3

Brain Teasers

1. What runs East and West, North and South, has teeth, but no mouth?

    Answer: A saw.

2. A woman was sitting in her hotel room when she heard a knock at the door. When she opened it, there was a man she had never seen before. And then he said, "Oops, I thought this was my room" and then left. When he left, the woman called the hotel security. Why?

Answer: Because no one ever knocks on the door of their hotel room. They simply use their keys to enter.

3. What starts and ends with "T" and is filled with "T"?

    Answer: A teapot.

4. What gets wetter and wetter the more it dries?

    Answer: A towel.

5. When is a Zero greater than a Nine?

    Answer: When we're talking about temperature. Zero Celsius is greater than Nine Fahrenheit. 0 Celsius > 9 Fahrenheit

6. What did one sleepy pair of underpants say to another pair of underpants?

    Answer: I'm going to take a brief nap!

7. What did the windmill say to the rock star?

    Answer: I'm a big fan!!

8. Why was the king only a foot tall?

Answer: Because he was a ruler!!

9. What five-letter word becomes shorter when you add 2 letters to it?

Answer: Short

10. Why did the boy bury his flashlight?

Answer: Because the batteries died.

11. What car doesn't have wheels, tires, windows, a windshield, an engine or a steering wheel?

Answer: A carpenter

12. What man doesn't have eyes, ears, arms, legs, a mouth or hands?

Answer: A manhole

13. What type of tree has fur (sounds like fir)?

Answer: A Douglas Fir

14. Which travels faster? Hot or Cold?

Answer: Hot. Because you can catch a cold.

15. Mr. Blue lives in the Blue House. Mr. Pink lives in the pink house. Mr. Black lives in the black house. Mr. Brown lives in the brown house. Who lives in the white house?

    Answer: The President.

16. What is something you'll never see again?

    Answer: Yesterday

17. A business owner, a doctor and a hat maker were walking down the street. Who had the biggest hat?

    Answer: The one with the biggest head.

18. Who is the fastest runner in the whole world?

    Answer: Adam. Because he was the first in the human race.

19. I have keys but no keyholes or locks. I have space, but no room. You can enter, but can't go outside. What am I?

    Answer: A computer keyboard.

20. If a blue house is made out of blue bricks, a yellow house is made out of yellow bricks, and a pink house is made out of pink bricks, what is a greenhouse made of?

Answer: Glass

21. What belongs to you, but others use it more than you do?

Answer: Your name.

22. You will throw me away when you want to use me. You will take me in when you don't want to use me. What am I?

Answer: An anchor

23. I have no life, but I can die. What am I?

Answer: A battery

24. We see it once in a year, twice in a week, but never in a day. What is it?

Answer: The letter e.

25. It is round on both sides but high in the middle. What is it?

Answer: Ohio

26. You can hear it, but not touch it nor see it. What is it?

Answer: Your voice.

27. It has one eye, but cannot see. What is it?

Answer: A needle

28. You can catch it but not throw it. What is it?

Answer: A cold

29. The more you take away from it the bigger it becomes. What is it?

Answer: A hole

30. What track should cars, bikes or trains not go on?

Answer: A TRACK-tor (tractor)

31. What nut isn't a nut like a peanut, hazelnut, almond, walnut, cashew nut or Brazilian nut?

Answer: A coconut

32. People buy me to eat, but never eat me. What am I?

Answer: A plate. Or utensils like a spoon, a fork, or a knife.

33. I will always come, but I'll never arrive today?

Answer: Tomorrow

34. What is so delicate that saying its name breaks it?

Answer: Silence.

35. What is the longest word in the dictionary?

Answer: Smiles. Because there's a mile in between each "s"

36. What could get broken without being touched or held?

Answer: A promise

37. You can keep it, but only after giving it to someone else. What is it?

Answer: Your word

38. When I'm young, I'm tall. And when I'm old, I'm short. What am I?

Answer: A candle

39. If you give me water, I will die. What am I?

Answer: Fire

40. I have cities, but no people live in those cities. I have forests but no trees and animals. I have rivers but no water. What am I?

Answer: A map

41. What state in the United States would kids who like to jump, run, play and move their bodies a lot, want to move to?

Answer: Kinetic-ut (Connecticut)

42. What state in the U.S. has the most baby pigs?

Answer: New ham-(p)-shire.

43. If April showers bring May flowers, what do May flowers bring?

Answer: Pilgrims

44. What has a head but never talks, what can run but never walks, what has a bed but never sleeps, and has a bank but no money nor an ATM that beeps?

Answer: A river

45. There was a man driving a truck. His truck lights weren't on. The moon was not out. In front of him was a woman crossing the street. How did he see her?

Answer: It was in the middle of a sunny day.

46. A man was cleaning the windows of a 20-storey building. He slipped and fell off his ladder, but didn't get hurt? How could this be?

    Answer: He fell off only from the second step.

47. Three men were in a boat. It capsized. Only two of them got their hair wet. Why?

    Answer: One was bald.

48. Why can't your head be 12 inches long?

    Answer: Because then it would be a foot!

49. Why did the student eat his homework?

    Answer: Because his teacher told him it was a piece of cake.

50. What did the tree say to the wind?

    Answer: Leaf me alone!

51. Why is 6 afraid of 7?

    Answer: Because 7 ate 9. ("ate" is a homonym of "eight" 8)

52. Where do you learn to make banana splits?

    Answer: At sundae school.

53. What two things can you never eat for breakfast?

    Answer: Lunch and dinner!

54. You can serve it, but never eat it. What is it?

    Answer: A tennis ball

55. What can you catch but not throw?

    Answer: A cold.

56. What starts with a P, ends with an E, and has thousands of letters?

    Answer: Post Office

57. You draw a line. Now without touching it, how do you make this line longer?

Answer: You draw a shorter one right next to it. Then the first line becomes the longer line.

58. What is so delicate that saying its name breaks it?

    Answer: Silence.

59. It has a neck but no head, and it wears a cap. What is it?

    Answer: A bottle

60. What kind of tree can you hold in your hand?

    Answer: A palm

61. A truck driver is going opposite traffic on a one-way street. A police officer spots him, but doesn't stop him. Why?

    Answer: The truck driver is walking!

62. A young lady is sitting in a house at night that has no lights at all. There are no candles or lamps around, and yet she is reading. How?

Answer: She is blind and is reading Braille.

63. The one who made it didn't want it. The one who bought it never used it. The one who used it didn't even see it. What is it?

Answer: A coffin

64. What goes up and down but never moves?

Answer: Temperature

65. What did the baseball glove say to the baseball?

Answer: Catch you later!

66. What did the beach say when the tide came in?

Answer: Long time, no sea!

67. How many months have 28 days?

Answer: All of them!

68. Two mothers and two daughters went out to eat burgers. Everyone ate one burger, but only a total of three burgers were eaten in all. How is this possible?

Answer: They were a grandmother, a mother and daughter.

69. Forward I am very heavy, but backward I am not. What am I?

Answer: Ton

70. You have a five-gallon bucket, a three-gallon bucket with and as much water as you need. But you don't have any other measuring devices. How would you fill the five-gallon bucket with exactly four gallons of water?

Answer: Fill the five-gallon bucket all the way up. Pour it into the three-gallon bucket until it is full. Empty the three-gallon bucket. Pour the remaining two gallons into the three-gallon bucket. Fill the five-gallon bucket all the way up, then finish filling the three-gallon bucket, leaving four gallons in the five-gallon bucket.

CHAPTER 4

Tongue Twisters

Say each tongue twister five (5) times speedily, without pausing.

1. Boy boat boy boat boy boat boy boat boy boat

2. Toy boat toy boat toy boat toy boat toy boat

3. Toy boat boy toy boat boy toy boat boy toy boat boy toy boat boy

4. Kitchen chicken kitchy-koo

5. Catch a kitchen chickadee

6. She sells seashells by the seashore.

7. Peter Piper picked a peck of pickled peppers. A peck of pickled peppers Peter Piper picked. If Peter Piper picked a peck of

pickled peppers, where's the peck of pickled peppers Peter Piper picked.

8. Sally slipped on her slippery slipper. Slippery slipper Sally slipped on.

9. Geese gaggled and giggled away. Gaggling geese giggled away. Giggling geese gaggled away. Geese gaggled and giggled away. Gaggling geese giggled away. Giggling geese gaggled away.

10. Chewy chooses Chinese chocolate chews.

11. Chester chews choice chocolates and cheese churned by champs.

12. Sheena leads, Sheila needs.

13. Lovey-dovey, lovely duvet (pronounced du-vey)

14. Clean clams crammed in clean.

15. Five frantic frogs fled from fifty fierce fishes.

16. He threw three balls through trees.

17. Scissors sizzle, thistles sizzle, tussles twizzle sizzle.

18. Klippety-klop clipped the lopsided Klondike.

19. Kloppety-klip clack Klippety-kloppety-clap.

20. She chills shells she'll sell.

CHAPTER 5

Knock-knock Jokes

Everyone enjoys knock-knock jokes. See if you can memorize some of these to ask your friends and family. You will all have loads of fun!!

1. Will you remember me in a minute?

    Yes, of course.
    Will you remember me in an hour?
    Yes.
    Will you remember me in a day?
    Yes.
    Knock-knock.
    Who's there?
    What, you didn't remember me?!!

2. Knock-knock.

   Who's there?
   Horsh.
   Horsh-who?
   Let's play a Horsh-who (horseshoe) game!

3. Knock-knock.

   Who's there?
   Cow says
   Cow says who?
   No, no. A cow says moo!!

4. Knock-knock.

   Who's there?
   Chair.
   Chair who?
   Chair-y (cherry) pie is one of my favorite desserts!

5. Knock-knock.

   Who's there?
   Chicken.
   Chicken who?
   We're chicken (checking) out the library books now.

6. Knock-knock.

   Who's there?
   Circus.

Circus who?
This is yours, sir -- 'cus (circus) my Dad gave it to you.

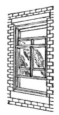

7. Knock-knock.

    Who's there?
    Window
    Window who?
    Window we eat, Mom? (When do we eat, Mom?)

8. Knock-knock.

    Who's there?
    Atch.
    Atch who? (sounds like a sneeze)
    Bless you!

9. Knock-knock.

    Who's there?
    Thank.
    Thank who? (sounds like Thank you)
    You're welcome!

10. Knock-knock.

    Who's there?
    Doris.
    Doris who?
    Doris (door is) locked, that's why I had to knock.

11. Knock-knock.

    Who's there?
    Window
    Window who?
    Window we go on vacation? (When do we go on vacation?)
    Or: Window we get to our destination? (When do we get to our destination?)

12. Knock-knock.

    Who's there?
    Butter.
    Butter who?
    I butter not tell you, it's a surprise.

13. Knock-knock.

    Who's there?
    Howard.
    Howard who?
    Howard he know? (sounds like "How would he know?")

14. Knock-knock.

Who's there?
Dwayne.
Dwayne who?
Dwayne (drain) the tub! I need to find my toy pebbles!

15. Knock-knock.

Who's there?
Justin.
Justin who?
You're Justin time for dinner!!

16. Knock-knock.

Who's there?
Orange.
Orange who?
Orange you glad we're friends?

17. Knock-knock.

Who's there?
Gorilla.
Gorilla who?
Would you please Gorilla (grill) me a cheese sandwich, Dad?

18.   Knock-knock.

Who's there?
Lettuce.
Lettuce who?
Lettuce in, it's freezing out here!

19.   Knock-knock.

Who's there?
Olive.
Olive who?
Olive (I live) just down the street from you.

20.   Knock-knock.

Who's there?
Freeze.
Freeze who?
Freeze (sounds like For he's) a jolly good fellow, freeze a jolly good fellow, freeze a jolly good fellow, that nobody can deny.
(Song)

21. Knock-knock.

    Who's there?
    Owls.
    Owls who?
    You're right, they do!!

22. Knock-knock.

    Who's there?
    Butter.
    Butter who?
    Butter (sounds like Better) get your
    raincoat, it looks like rain!

23. Knock-knock.

    Who's there?
    Boo.
    Boo who?
    Don't cry, it's just a knock-knock joke!

24. Knock-knock.

    Who's there?
    Cows.
    Cows who?
    No, that's wrong, cow's moo!!

25. Knock-knock.

    Who's there?
    Dora.
    Dora who?

Dora's (sounds like "Door is") locked, would you please open it for me?

26. Knock-knock.

    Who's there?
    Mary and Abby
    Mary and Abby who?
    Mary Christmas and an Abby new year to you!!

27. Knock-knock.

    Who's there?
    Twig
    Twig who?
    Twig-onometry isn't one of my favorite subjects.
    [OR Twig or Treat!!]

28. Knock-knock.

    Who's there?
    Ohio.
    Ohio who?
    O, hi...oh how are you?

29. Knock-knock.

Who's there?
Bless.
Bless who?
I didn't sneeze!!

30. Knock-knock.

Who's there?
Wooden shoe.
Wooden shoe who?
Wooden-shoe (Wouldn't you) like to get some ice cream with me?

31. Knock-knock.

Who's there?
Stop watch.
Stopwatch who?
Stopwatch you're doing and help me please!!

32. Knock-knock.

Who's there?
Dishes
Dishes who?
Dishes a great place to have a picnic!!

33. Knock-knock.

Who's there?
Yah!
Yah who?

Did I just hear a cowboy nearby?

34. Knock-knock.

   Who's there?
   I am.
   I am who?
   Do you not know who you are?

35. Knock-knock.

   Who's there?
   Ear.
   Ear who?
   Ear is your present…happy birthday!!

36. Knock-knock.

   Who's there?
   Hebrews.
   Hebrews who?
   Hebrews the best coffee in this area!!

37. Knock-knock.

   Who's there?
   Dots.
   Dots who?
   Dots my Mom and Dad over there. Let me
   introduce you to them.

38. Knock-knock.

   Who's there?

Handsome.
Handsome who?
Handsome money to me, please -- there's
an ice cream truck coming by and I want a
popsicle!!

39. Knock-knock.

Who's there?
Champ.
Champ who?
Champ-poo your hair, please -- it's getting
dirty.

40. Knock-knock.

Who's there?
Isabelle.
Isabelle who?
Isabelle ringing? Or am I hearing things?

41. Knock-knock.

Who's there?
Claire.
Claire who?
Claire the hallway for a huge delivery!

42. Knock-knock.

Who's there?
Abby.
Abby who?

Abby birthday to you!

43. Knock-knock.

    Who's there?
    Anita.
    Anita who?
    Anita borrow a pencil, please.

44. Knock-knock.

    Who's there?
    Figs.
    Figs who?
    Figs your doorbell, please, ok?

45. Knock-knock.

    Who's there?
    Ya.
    Ya who?
    Well, I'm excited to see you, too!

46. Knock-knock.

    Who's there?
    Water.
    Water who?
    Water you doing in my house?

47. Knock-knock.

    Who's there?
    Ima.
    Ima who?

Ima gonna tickle you!

48. Knock-knock.

Who's there?
Amy.
Amy who?
Amy fraid I've forgotten! (I'm afraid I've forgotten!)

49. Knock-knock.

Who's there?
Alpaca.
Alpaca who?
Alpaca the suitcase, you load the trunk!

50. Knock-knock.

Who's there?
Cash.
Cash who?
No thanks, I'd prefer some peanuts please!

CHAPTER 6

Star Wars Riddles and Knock-knock Jokes

1.   Why is Yoda (Star Wars character) such a good gardener?

      Answer: Because he has a green thumb.

2.   Why did Darth Vader cross the road?

      Answer: To get to the dark side.

3.   Why is Yoda such a newbie at things?

      Answer: Because he is so green.

4. Darth Vader to the audience: How did Han win the limbo contest?

Answer: He went So-lo. (sounds like "So low")

5. Knock-knock.

Who's there?
Jack
Jack-who?
Jakku!! That's the planet where Ankur Thug lived!!

6. Knock-knock.

Who's there?
Droid
Droid who?
Droid up (dried up) creeks are common in the summer.

7. What is one of the favorite Star Wars dates of the year?

Answer: It's on May 4. Because Star Wars fans greet each other: May the Fourth be with you!!

CHAPTER 7

Your Amazing BONUS! Sea Creature Word Search

```
H T J H X V U O I W T D X I U J F
S S N W P N M P Z U E K W P H N F
I H S I F E Y E L E R R A B Y E Z
F S N W Y I Z V W A L R U S E T T
N O O S H H D A L O D L P R X G Q
O C X K P A E O V Z Z F L M I F N
G Q X U K S L L L I E A V A P I G
A J S M I X W E S P R R N P H R S
R X B W K F E E S R H T A C C D E
D V K F O J A R O S I I R B L C A
Q G U M Z T D C B S T U N R O C L
I E B Z U I F L O Y A A W R W C I
C N H R U Q M P P E Y C R S N D O
A G T Q U M O Q S V N D G F F R N
L L S Y W D J F W M C K S Z I V L
E S O C T O P U S H M S C X S S Z
K R A H S D A E H R E M M A H S H
```

ClownFish	BarrelEyeFish	Dragonfish
GiantIsopod	Walrus	Seaweed
Squid	Octopus	Whale
StarFish	SeaLion	Dolphin
CorralReef	SeaUrchin	HammerheadShark
SeaTurtle		

Answers to Your Amazing BONUS! Sea Creature Word Search

Sea Creatures

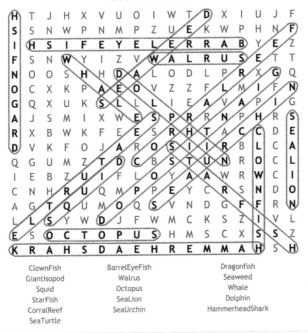

H	T	J	H	X	V	U	O	I	W	T	D	X	I	U	J	F
S	S	N	W	P	N	M	P	Z	U	E	K	W	P	H	N	F
I	H	S	I	F	E	Y	E	L	E	R	R	A	B	Y	E	Z
F	S	N	W	Y	I	Z	V	W	A	L	R	U	S	E	T	T
N	O	O	S	H	H	D	A	L	O	D	L	P	R	X	G	Q
O	C	X	K	P	A	E	O	V	Z	Z	F	L	M	I	F	N
G	Q	X	U	K	S	L	L	L	I	E	A	V	A	P	I	G
A	J	S	M	I	X	W	E	S	P	R	R	N	P	H	R	S
R	X	B	W	K	F	E	E	S	R	H	T	A	C	C	D	E
D	V	K	F	O	J	A	R	O	S	I	I	R	B	L	C	A
Q	G	U	M	Z	T	D	C	B	S	T	U	N	R	O	C	L
I	E	B	Z	U	I	F	L	O	Y	A	A	W	R	W	C	I
C	N	H	R	U	Q	M	P	P	E	Y	C	R	S	N	D	O
A	G	T	Q	U	M	O	Q	S	V	N	D	G	F	F	R	N
L	L	S	Y	W	D	J	F	W	M	C	K	S	Z	I	V	L
E	S	O	C	T	O	P	U	S	H	M	S	C	X	S	S	Z
K	R	A	H	S	D	A	E	H	R	E	M	M	A	H	S	H

ClownFish	BarrelEyeFish	Dragonfish
GiantIsopod	Walrus	Seaweed
Squid	Octopus	Whale
StarFish	SeaLion	Dolphin
CorralReef	SeaUrchin	HammerheadShark
SeaTurtle		

About the Authors

Jackie Morey is a multiple-time #1 International Bestselling Author, Book Writing and Publishing Coach, Wife, and Mother of two children. When she's not homeschooling her kiddos, she enjoys traveling abroad with her Husband, especially to white sand, warm beaches with sky-colored water in the Philippines, playing chess with her children, having conversations over coffee with friends, watching movies, reading, and enjoying food from many different countries.

She has coached hundreds of people from all walks of life – to help them write and publish their books – business books, devotionals, non-fiction topic books, legacy books, Children's books and fiction books. She especially enjoys helping those who've dreamt of becoming authors for decades, to finally write the stories of their lives, their unique message, their life lessons, and business books.

Jackie has launched dozens of select Premier Clients from zero idea to Bestselling Authors!

She and her wonderful Husband Jim, have concocted their "secret sauce" and used this to help writers become authors, and authors become Bestselling Authors.

If you're interested in writing your business book, your Legacy book, a fiction book, a Children's book or any type of book series, connect with Jackie via email: CustomerStrategyAcademy @gmail.com and let her know what type of book you'd like to write.

Michael Morey is the eldest of two children to Jim and Jackie Morey. This is his first book. As of this publication, Michael is about to enter 4TH Grade. He enjoys bike riding, swimming, solving Rubik's cubes, climbing trees, playing chess, adult coloring books, adult dot-to-dot books, creating art projects, drawing sea creatures, solving puzzles, reading, exchanging knock-knock jokes & riddles with his family and friends, building toys and watching movies.

Your BONUS for reading our book: Jackie and her business friend Jay Boyer did a webinar in November 2017 called "**How to Write and Publish a #1 Bestselling Children's Book in 7 Days or Less.**" Please go to this link to watch the Replay: http://bit.ly/ChildrensBookJackieMorey

Quick note: Although the Bonuses mentioned in the webinar have already *expired*, the webinar content is value-packed **and** as relevant today as it was then. If you've always wanted to write a Children's Book, **this** is the webinar to watch right now http://bit.ly/ChildrensBookJackieMorey

And whenever you're ready **and** are serious about writing your Children's book, invest in yourself and learn from Jay Boyer who's a Children's Book Bestselling Author http://bit.ly/cbf-jackie

PLEASE RATE OUR BOOK

We'd be honored if you would take a few moments to rate our book on Amazon.com.

A five-star rating and a short comment ("Fun to read!" or "Enjoyed it!") would be much appreciated. We welcome longer, positive comments as well.

If you feel like this book should be rated at three stars or fewer, please hold off posting your comments on Amazon. Instead, please send your feedback directly to me (Jackie), so that we can use it to improve the next edition. We're committed to providing the best value to our customers and readers, and your thoughts can make that possible.

You can reach me (Jackie) at CustomerStrategyAcademy@gmail.com.

Thank you so much!,

Jackie and Michael

Made in the USA
Las Vegas, NV
31 March 2021